by Jenna Lynn   illustrated by Abigail Dela Cruz

ROBYN HOOD

RIVALS

Spellbound
An Imprint of Magic Wagon
abdobooks.com

To my family, who have been my strongest supporters,
Dad, Mom, Zandra, Berna, Wowo, Mama and Tita Beth —ADC

For my family —JL

abdobooks.com

Printed in the United States of America, North Mankato, Minnesota.
092018
012019

**THIS BOOK CONTAINS
RECYCLED MATERIALS**

Written by Jenna Lynn
Illustrated by Abigail Dela Cruz
Edited by Bridget O'Brien
Design Contributors: Victoria Bates, Candice Keimig and Laura Mitchell

Library of Congress Control Number: 2018947814

Publisher's Cataloging-in-Publication Data

Names: Lynn, Jenna, author. | Dela Cruz, Abigail, illustrator.
Title: Rivals / by Jenna Lynn; illustrated by Abigail Dela Cruz.
Description: Minneapolis, Minnesota : Magic Wagon, 2019. | Series: Robyn Hood;
    book 2
Summary: When a rival gang comes to town and starts stealing from innocent people,
    master thief Robyn Hood must find a way to return the goods and give the gang a
    taste of their own medicine.
Identifiers: ISBN 9781532133770 (lib. bdg.) | ISBN 9781532134371 (ebook) | ISBN
    9781532134678 (Read-to-me ebook)
Subjects: LCSH: Stealing--Juvenile fiction. | Thieves--Juvenile fiction. | Retribution--
    Juvenile fiction. | Adventure stories--Juvenile fiction.
Classification: DDC [FIC]--dc23

TABLE OF CONTENTS

Chapter One

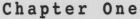

THE HAVOCS

Robyn Hood leaned against the workbench on the first floor of the **ABANDONED** warehouse she lived in. She was practicing a code-cracking drill on a BEAT-UP keypad.

"Almost got it . . ." the master

THIEF said.

Suddenly, the front door

FLEW open. Robyn's friends Silas,

Jasper, and Cole **BURST**

through. They were her loyal **SIDEKICKS**. Everyone called them the Hoods.

"Guys! I was this close to **cracking** that code!"

"Sorry, Robyn, but we've got **BIGGER** problems," Silas said.

"We heard YELLING at the train station," Jasper explained. "When we got to the platform, it was SMOKY. People said there had been an **EXPLOSION**, but no one saw what happened."

"Then a woman spotted her wallet at Mr. Grey's feet and accused him of **STEALING** it. Everyone started *ACCUSING* each other of setting everything up."

Robyn had a **GRIM** look on her face. "Sounds like the Havocs are in town."

Chapter Two

FIGHT AT THE MARKET

"Keep your **EYES** peeled and stay close," Robyn said. The Hoods entered Metropolis's open-air market.

"If the Havocs are around, they're sure to come here. Plenty of pockets to pick and goods to be *STOLEN*."

Once in a while a group of teenagers came to town to stir up **TROUBLE**, framing others for their crimes. They were known for their **NEON** Mohawks.

Robyn and the Hoods didn't **STEAL** from innocent people like the Havocs. They only took from bad guys to **HELP** people in need.

"Over there!" Cole pointed to a **FLASH** of bright orange across the market.

Robyn and the Hoods ran toward the **Havoc**, fighting through the crowd and **DODGING** carts. Finally, they reached the clearing where they had first SPOTTED him.

"He was just here!" Cole said in DISBELIEF. Whatever they may have seen, no Havoc was there now.

"SOMETHING doesn't feel right," Robyn said. The hairs on the back of her neck PRICKLED.

A **SHRIEK** rang across the market. A **crowd** was forming where Robyn and the Hoods had just come from. People were **YELLING** and shoving each other.

"You *STOLE* my bracelet, I know it! Just like you took Stella's wallet at the train station!" Mrs. Vol screamed at Mr. Grey.

"It wasn't me. It was Hops!" Mr. Grey said as he POINTED an *ACCUSING* finger at his neighbor.

"How dare you!" Mr. Hops YELLED.

Robyn shook her head as the **ACCUSATIONS** kept flying. She couldn't believe the Havocs had **tricked** her so easily. She scanned the market for signs of them.

A strawberry-blond braid

swinging in the wind caught her

eye. Robyn recognized the tall,

LANKY figure it belonged to.

It was the **mysterious** girl who kept showing up whenever there was TROUBLE. Could she have something to do with this?

Robyn **RAN** as fast as she could after the girl.

"**AH!**" Robyn cried as she tripped over an **OPEN** sewer grate.

She **STUMBLED**, but instead of continuing after the girl, Robyn paused to *examine* the grate.

"Robyn, what's going on?" The Hoods had just *CAUGHT* up to her.

"I think I know where the Havocs are hiding."

Chapter Three

INTO THE
SEWERS

"What was that?!" Cole yelped.
Rats skittered past Robyn and
the Hoods as they made their way
through the **GRIMY** sewer tunnels.

"They're just rats, just **RATS**,"
Cole mumbled to himself.

"Those are nothing compared to the **GIANT** ones that live down here," Jasper said.

"Giant ones?" Cole **gulped**.

"Oh yeah, as TALL as you on their hind legs," Silas chimed in.

"**Liars**," Cole said with a worried look on his face.

"Which way, boss?" Jasper asked Robyn. They had reached a fork in the **tunnel**. Robyn hesitated. Should they **split** up?

Then something SPARKLY
down the tunnel to the right
caught Robyn's EYE. "This way!"

Robyn and the Hoods crept down the **tunnel**. Sure enough, a treasure trove of *STOLEN* goods lay at the end: the bracelet, wallets, cell phones.

"*HURRY*, they could be back any minute," Robyn said. They collected the **VALUABLES** to return to their owners. "I have a plan."

Chapter Four

THE
SHOWDOWN

"Here they come."

The Havocs walked into

the **EMPTY** Metropolis market.

After returning the **STOLEN**

goods, the Hoods convinced

everyone to **STAY OUT**

of the market so they could

face the Havocs.

"So the **goody-goody** and her pathetic **SiDEKiCKS** thought they could take our stuff, huh?" Julius, the **leader** of the Havocs, gave Robyn an icy stare.

"You knew we wouldn't let you **GET AWAY** with this, Julius," Robyn said.

"Ah, yes, **silly** me. The girl who considers herself a 'master thief' doesn't actually understand the concept of *STEALING*. Let me explain. I take it. It's **MINE**. Pretty simple."

"Now," Julius continued. "I suggest you **RUNTS** give everything back to us before we make you."

The Havocs **cracked** their knuckles and sneered. Jasper yawned. "Am I boring you, **RUNT**?" Julius asked with a snarl.

"A *little* bit," Jasper admitted.

Julius and the other Havocs **LUNGED** for Jasper. They didn't notice the camouflaged *trip line* at their feet.

"**OOF!**" The Havocs toppled on each other.

Robyn and the Hoods *RACED* forward to tie them up, but as they got close, there was a loud **CRACK** of an explosion. Thick SMOKE spread through the market.

"They're . . . gonna . . . get
away," Robyn said between
COUGHS. She tried to get
her bearings, but her eyes **STUNG**
and she couldn't open them.

When the SMOKE cleared, the
Havocs were nowhere in *sight*.
Cole wanted to go after them.

"It's **NOT** worth it," Robyn replied. "We got everyone's **VALUABLES** back and that is what's important. We'll **FACE** the Havocs another day."